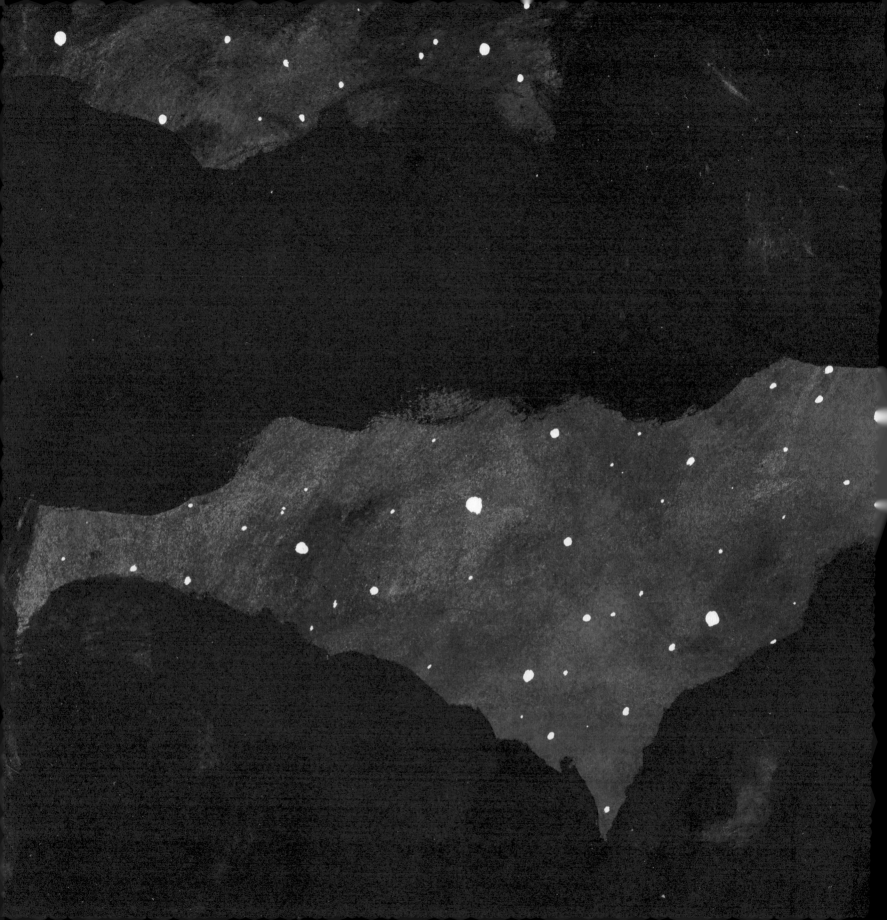

THE RED TIN BOX

THE RED TIN BOX

By Matthew Burgess

Illustrated by Evan Turk

chronicle books · san francisco

On her eighth birthday, when the sun
was peeking over the treetops

and everyone in the house
was still asleep,

Maude slipped outside
and across the wet grass
to the edge of the woods.

At the foot
of the flowering
dogwood,

in a soft spot
where she once found
a fallen nest,

the earth seemed to whisper,

"Here."

Maude dug and dug and dug
until the hole was deep enough
to hold a red tin box.

Only Maude knew
the treasures she placed
inside the box.

Only Maude heard
the words she said
as she buried it.

Far overhead,
the sun kissed the clouds pink,
an angle of geese honked excitedly,

and Maude made a promise to herself.

Maude grew

and grew

and grew,

as all children do . . .

She had a daughter of her own,

and she grew, too.

But Maude never forgot the red tin box.

In one corner of her mind,
    it glowed . . .

though one by one,

the treasures she had placed inside

slipped from her memory.

One November afternoon,
Maude was seized with a feeling—

a feeling like a bright spring sunrise.

The next day, Maude picked up
her granddaughter after school.

Together they turned east . . .

As they drove

and drove

and drove,

four towns over,

across the river she swam in as a girl,

past the road to the old schoolhouse,

Maude told Eve about the red tin box,

about the hole she dug beneath the dogwood,

about the promise she made
when she was eight years old.

"But what's inside the box?
How do you know it's still there?"

These were questions
Maude couldn't answer.

They sat quietly, side by side,
in worry and in wonder.

It was possible
they wouldn't find it.

So many years had passed.

But *there* was the dogwood
that Maude daydreamed under as a girl,
read books under, fell asleep in the grass under.

Holding her granddaughter's hand,
Maude walked the perimeter of the tree
until one spot seemed to whisper,

"Here."

They took turns
nudging the shovels
into the cold ground.

Digging was hard,
but with each small scoop
the dirt became a little bit softer

until suddenly . . .

the ring of a metallic *clink*!

Eve watched as her grandmother
lifted the treasures out,
examining them one by one:

a tiny toy elephant,
a marble like a tiger's eye,

an ancient piece of candy
wrapped in silver foil,

a costume mustache,
a small brown bottle,

a bird's nest woven with purple string,
and an iridescent ear-shaped shell.

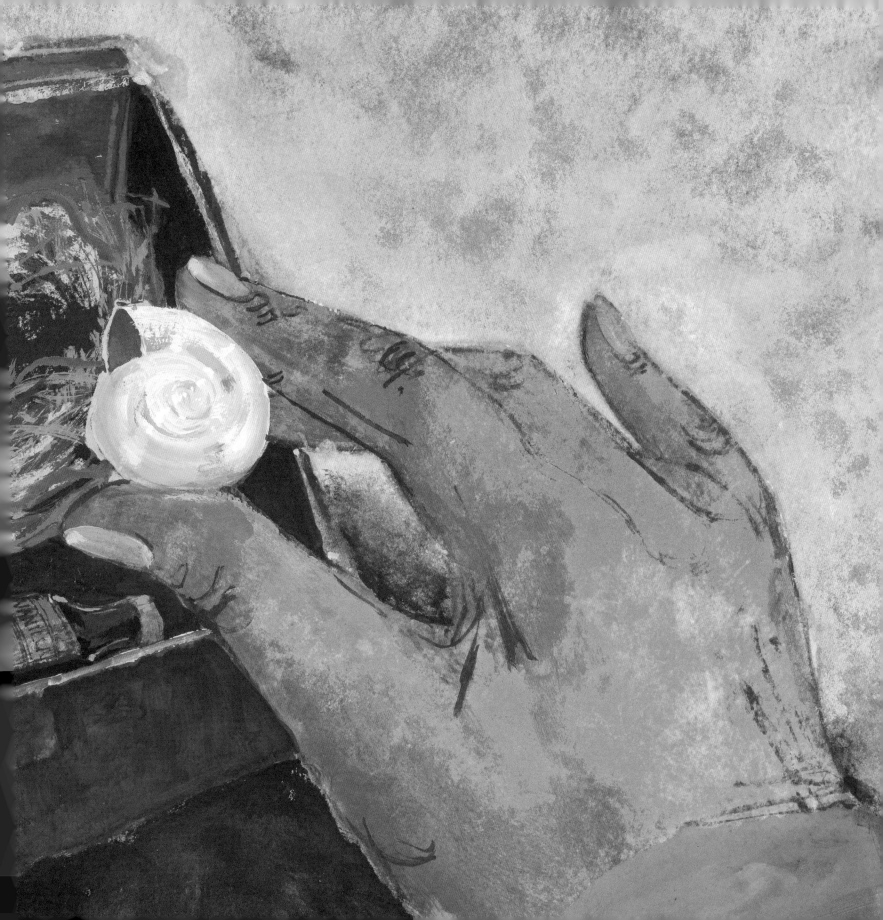

Once, Maude let out such a high-pitched "*HA!*"

that a dog in the distance began barking.

Maude told many stories on the drive home.

Sometimes Eve asked questions.

Sometimes she laughed when her grandmother laughed,

and it didn't bother her
when her grandmother cried . . .

Not one bit.

When they arrived,
Maude placed the red tin box
into her granddaughter's hands.

"This is for you."

Far overhead,

    the stars blinked,
        an angle of geese honked
           in the dusky dark,

and Eve, seized with a feeling,
made a promise to herself.

Library of Congress Cataloging-in-Publication Data

Names: Burgess, Matthew, author. | Turk, Evan, illustrator.
Title: The red tin box / by Matthew Burgess ; illustrated by Evan Turk.
Description: San Francisco : Chronicle Books LLC, 2023. | Audience: Ages
  5-8. | Audience: Grades K-1. | Summary: On her eighth birthday Maude
  buries a red tin box with some special treasures at the foot of a
  flowering dogwood tree and makes a promise to herself—and many years
  later she and her granddaughter travel to her childhood home to dig it
  up and pass it on.
Identifiers: LCCN 2022025704 | ISBN 9781452179735 (hardcover) | ISBN
  9781452179872 (ebook) | ISBN 9781797223209 (kindle edition) | ISBN
  9781797223216 (ebook other)
Subjects: LCSH: Time capsules—Juvenile fiction. | Grandmothers—Juvenile
  fiction. | Grandparent and child—Juvenile fiction. | CYAC: Time
  capsules—Fiction. | Grandmothers—Fiction. | Grandparent and
  child—Fiction. | LCGFT: Picture books.
Classification: LCC PZ7.1.B8743 Re 2023 | DDC 813.6
  [Fic]—dc23/eng/20220601
LC record available at https://lccn.loc.gov/2022025704

Manufactured in China.

Design by Ryan Hayes.
Typeset in Albra Text.
The illustrations in this book were rendered in gouache.

10 9 8 7 6 5 4 3 2 1

Chronicle Books LLC
680 Second Street
San Francisco, California 94107

Chronicle Books—we see things differently.
Become part of our community at www.chroniclekids.com.

For Celeste and V. — M. B.
To my Gamma, Nana, and Oma. — E. T.